Trevor knew that the man in the
green coat was going to stick a knife
into him. He was going to cut open
Trevor's belly and take out his appendix.

'What do you do with them?' asked Trevor.
'With what?' said the doctor.
'Appendixcs and tonsils and things.'
'Burn them,' said the doctor.
'I want to keep mine in a jar,' said Trevor.
And he did, until …

…the appendix broke loose and really crazy things
started to happen

had to be together.

A WACKY TALE OF
AND HIS APPENDIX

WIZARD OF WEIRD,
PAUL JENNINGS

Other books by Paul Jennings

Unreal
Unbelievable
Quirky Tails
Uncanny
Unbearable
Unmentionable
Undone
Uncovered
Unseen
Round the Twist

The Cabbage Patch Fib
The Cabbage Patch War
(illustrated by Craig Smith)

The Paw Thing
Singenpoo Strikes Again
Singenpoo Shoots Through
(illustrated by Keith McEwan)

The Gizmo
The Gizmo Again
Come Back Gizmo
Sink the Gizmo
(illustrated by Keith McEwan)

Wicked!
Deadly!
(with Morris Gleitzman)

Picture Books
Spooner or Later, Duck for Cover and *Freeze a Crowd*
(all with Ted Greenwood and Terry Denton)

Sucked in...

Paul Jennings

Illustrated by
Terry Denton

PUFFIN BOOKS

Puffin Books
Penguin Books Australia Ltd
487 Maroondah Highway, PO Box 257
Ringwood, Victoria 3134, Australia
Penguin Books Ltd
Harmondsworth, Middlesex, England
Penguin Putnam Inc.
375 Hudson Street, New York, New York 10014, USA
Penguin Books Canada Limited
10 Alcorn Avenue, Toronto, Ontario, Canada, M4V 3B2
Penguin Books (N.Z.) Ltd
Cnr Rosedale and Airborne Roads, Albany, Auckland, New Zealand
Penguin Books (South Africa) (Pty) Ltd
5 Watkins Street, Denver Ext 4, 2094, South Africa
Penguin Books India (P) Ltd
11, Community Centre, Panchsheel Park, New Delhi 110 017, India

First published as 'Together Again' in *The Paul Jennings Superdiary 1996*
by Penguin Books Australia 1995
This revised and illustrated edition published by Penguin Books Australia, 2000
and in the UK by Puffin Books, 2001

10 9 8 7 6 5 4 3 2

Designed by George Dale, Penguin Design Studio

Typeset in 12.5/15 pt. Palatino by Midland Typesetters, Maryborough, Victoria

Made and printed by Griffin Press. Adelaide, South Australia

Penguin Books Ltd, UK ISBN 0 14 131199 1.

National Library of Australia
Cataloguing-in-Publication data:

Jennings, Paul, 1943- .
Sucked in.

ISBN 0 14 131066 9.

I. Denton, Terry, 1950- . II. Title. III. Title:
The Paul Jennings superdiary 1996.

A823.3

www.puffin.com.au
www.puffin.co.uk

For our friend
Ted Greenwood,
a master storyteller,
great companion
and constant inspiration
to us both.

P.J. and T.D.

The jar has something floating around inside it. Something awful. Something grey and fleshy. Something foul. Something not alive but not dead either.

A shiver goes down my spine. I wish I could stop peering at the thing in the jar.

But I can't.

The other kids are staring too. Every eye looks at the jar on the desk.

'Okay,' says the new teacher. 'Write a story about this.'

A groan goes up.

The thing in the jar is just another way of getting us to write stories while the teacher cleans out the cupboard.

He probably made it out of a bit of leather or something.

'I can't think of anything,' says Mary Jo.

'Neither can I,' says Helen Chung.

I couldn't think of anything either.

Mr Denton gives a grin. 'Okay,' he says. 'I will make up a story first. That will give you an idea of the sort of thing I want. Then you can have a go.'

This sounds much better.

*We all settle down to listen to Mr Denton.
But we don't look at him.*

*We gaze at the thing in
the jar. It floats there,
silently.*

Mr Denton begins his story.

ONE

Trevor knew that the man in the green coat was going to stick a knife into him. Well, a scalpel anyway. He was going to cut open Trevor's belly and take out his appendix.

'What do you do with them?' asked Trevor as he lay on the operating table.

'With what?' said the doctor.

'Appendixes and tonsils and things. After you cut them out.'

'Burn them,' said the doctor. 'In an incinerator.'

'I want to keep mine,' said Trevor. 'I don't want you to burn it.'

6

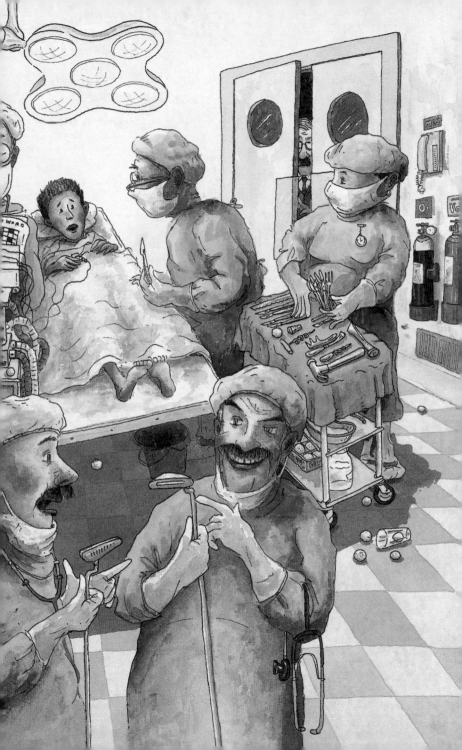

The doctor looked at the nurse from behind his mask. He wasn't too sure what to say. The nurse nodded. 'Okay,' said the doctor. 'I'll put it in a jar for you.'

He pricked Trevor's arm with a needle and the room started to spin.

'Good,' mumbled Trevor, just before everything turned black. 'We must always be together – me and my appendix.'

When Trevor woke up he had stitches across his belly. And a jar next to his bed with something grey and fleshy floating inside it.

Even though his stomach hurt he gave a grin. His appendix might be out. But it wasn't gone.

He picked up the jar and stared at it. 'You're never leaving me,' he said. 'Never. We must always be together.'

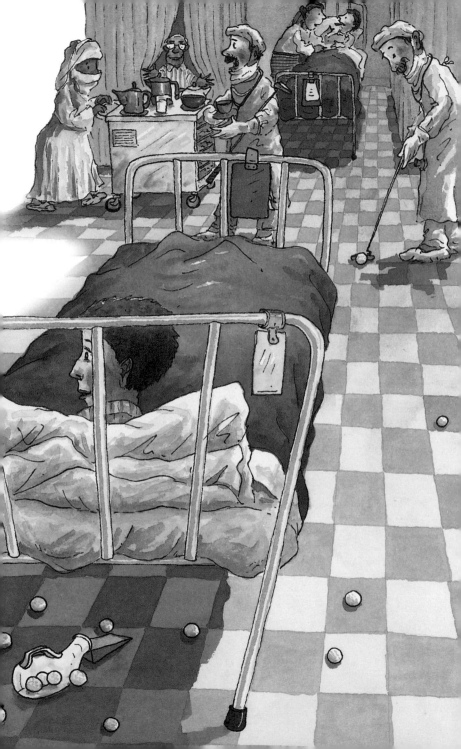

When he got home from hospital Trevor put the jar in a safe place and went up to his room.

He took off his dressing-gown and climbed into bed. Then he snuggled down and closed his eyes.

He was just starting to drift off to sleep when a terrible scream came from the kitchen.

Trevor hobbled down the stairs as fast as he could. He found his mother staring into the fridge.

'What's up?' he yelled.

'I'm not having that revolting appendix in there,' said his mother. 'It's digusting.'

'It's not disgusting. It's part of me. Just like my eyes and brains and that. If you don't like my appendix you don't like me.'

'What have you put it in the fridge for?' she said.

'So it doesn't go bad,' said Trevor.

'It won't go bad, Trevor. It's in formalin. The liquid preserves it.'

Trevor looked at the appendix in the jar. 'It's best to be on the safe side,' he said. 'It's part of me. I can't let anything happen to it.'

'Well, it's not going in the fridge,' said his mother. 'Someone might think it's a pickle and eat it.'

Trevor nodded. 'You're right,' he said thoughtfully. 'We couldn't have that. Are you sure it won't go bad?'

'I'm sure,' said his mum.

'Good,' said Trevor. 'I'll be able to take it to school with me then. Me and my appendix. We must always be together.'

His mum just sighed and shook her head.

THREE

So the appendix went to school.

Trevor dumped the jar down on his desk. Everyone stopped talking.

Every eye looked at the jar. Some kids gasped. But most kids just stared. They stared and stared and stared. None of them could stop looking at it.

The jar had something floating around in it. Something awful. Something grey and fleshy. Something foul. Something not alive but not dead either.

A shiver went down every spine. Every spine except Trevor's.

'It's my appendix,' he said. 'Where I go it goes.'

14

The class was amazed. No one had ever seen an appendix before.

'You'd better leave this on my desk, Trevor,' said his teacher, Mr Birtle. 'No one seems to be able to stop looking at it. We'll never get any work done this way.'

Actually it was Mr Birtle who couldn't stop looking at the jar. He seemed to be mesmerised by it.

'Are you sure this is an appendix, Trevor? I could swear that it was alive. I thought I saw it move.'

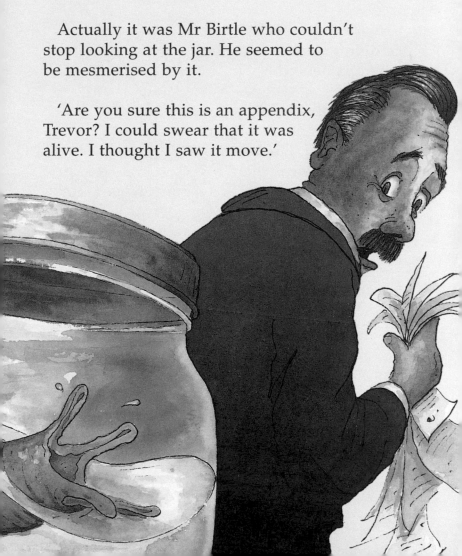

Everyone stared at the appendix. It swirled slowly in the yellow liquid.

'Go down to the library, Trevor, and ask for an anatomy book,' said Mr Birtle. 'I want to see just what an appendix looks like.'

Trevor didn't really want to go. He didn't want to leave his appendix behind.

As he walked slowly down the stairs his hands began to feel sweaty. His heart thumped loudly. His head hurt.

He wanted to turn around and run back to the class. He wanted to grab his jar and hold it close to his face. 'We must always be together,' he said to himself. He hurried to the library and started to search for an anatomy book.

Back in the classroom Mr Birtle gasped. The appendix was definitely moving around. Like an angry goldfish, it circled inside the jar.

And in the library Trevor also circled between the shelves like an angry goldfish.

Finally he found what he was looking for. He grabbed the anatomy book and rushed back to the classroom.

Mr Birtle looked up as Trevor entered. 'It's angry,' he said to Trevor. 'It's swimming around and around.'

Trevor rushed over to the jar and peered in. The appendix just floated there. Hardly moving.

A strange look came over Mr Birtle's face. 'It *was* moving,' he said. 'It stopped when you came back. Go and stand outside the door, Trevor.'

'I don't want to,' said Trevor. 'I don't want to leave it. We must always be together.'

Mr Birtle tightened his lips. 'It doesn't want you to leave either,' he said. 'Go and stand outside the door – it's only for a moment.'

Trevor did as he was told.

He left the room and stood outside.
His hands were sweaty. His head hurt.
His heart pumped heavily.

He stared in the window
and gasped.

The appendix was rushing around inside the jar. It was leaping out of the yellow formalin like a trout on a fisherman's line.

The students all took several steps backwards. They were scared. Something weird was happening.

Trevor rushed back in and grabbed the jar. Straight away the appendix calmed down and simply floated in the formalin.

'We'll give it one more try,' said Mr Birtle. 'Trevor, I want you to go outside, cross the road and go into the milk bar. Count to twenty and then come back.'

Trevor put down the jar and walked slowly out

of the door. He trembled as he made his way across the road. The further away he got the worse his head hurt. He wrung his wet hands together. He put his hand on his thumping heart. With shaking legs he walked into the shop and closed the door behind him.

A roar came from the school as thirty people screamed out together.

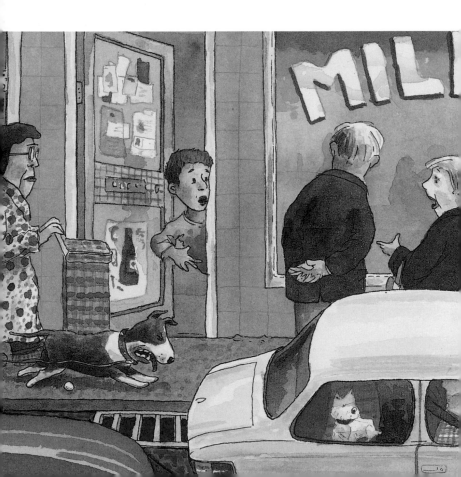

Trevor didn't even
feel his feet touch the
ground. He almost flew
back to the classroom.

'We must be together,'
he screamed.

He fell into the room. Everyone was out of their seat. Backing away from the appendix in horror.

They were all terrified.

Even Mr Birtle.

The appendix was leaping up and down inside the jar, banging against the lid. It sounded like bullets from a crazy machine-gun. The lid trembled under the strain.

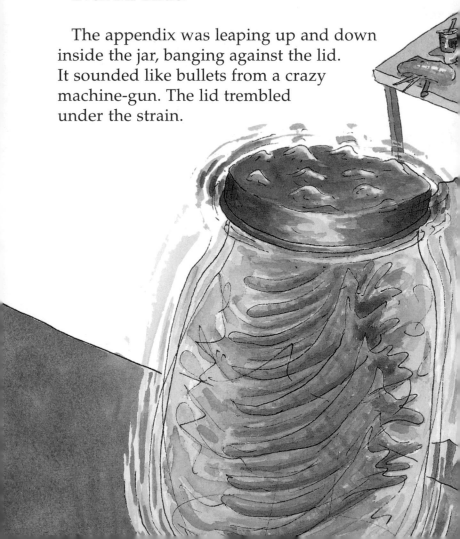

Trevor rushed over and grabbed the jar. The appendix fell still. It circled quietly in its fluid. Content.

Trevor smiled at it. Happy. 'You'll never leave me.' he said. 'Never.'

Mr Birtle strode to the front of the class. 'I'll have to take that, Trevor,' he said, snatching the jar. 'Something strange is going on. This could be dangerous.'

'Okay,' said Trevor with a grin. 'If that's what you want.' He turned and walked to the door. The class started to scream in panic as the appendix once again drilled away at the lid.

'Come back,' shouted Mr Birtle. He thrust the jar into Trevor's hands.

'Thanks,' said Trevor. The appendix circled happily. 'We must always be together,' said Trevor.

Just then the bell rang and the class headed out for lunch. 'You wait here, Trevor,' said Mr Birtle. 'I'm going to get the principal.'

FOUR

Trevor looked at his appendix. 'They are going to take you away,' he said. 'They won't let you stay with with me, that's for sure.'

The appendix bobbed up and down. It seemed to agree.

'We have to get out of here,' said Trevor. 'We must always be together.' He clasped the jar to his chest and sneaked down the stairs. He crept along the corridor and out of the back door.

Suddenly a hand fell on his shoulder. It was Mr Birtle and the principal.

'I'll have that,' said the principal. He grabbed the jar from Trevor's shaking hands.

Straight away the appendix began to drill up and down at the lid. It hammered so fast that it was just a blur inside the bottle.

'Get it out of the school,' yelled Mr Birtle. 'It could attack the children.'

'No,' screamed Trevor. 'Give it back. Give it back.'

Mr Birtle grabbed Trevor by the arms and held him tight.

'Come back, come back,' screamed Trevor. But it was no use. His appendix had gone.

The principal ran for it, carrying the vibrating jar in his trembling fingers.

He threw the jar onto the back seat of his car and sped out of the school gate.

The principal's hands shook on the steering wheel. He looked over his shoulder at the appendix which was furiously attacking the lid of the jar.

At any moment the top might burst. What then? The whole thing could explode like a bomb.

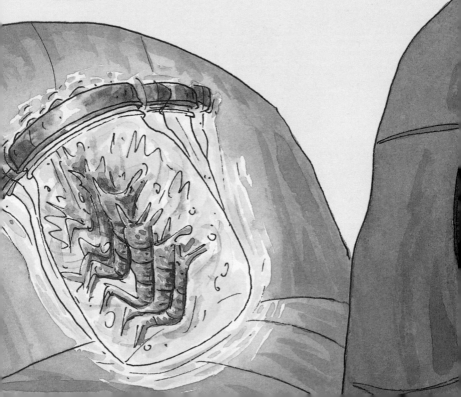

He jammed his foot on the brake pedal. Then he grabbed the jar and placed it on the footpath.

Shaking with fear, the principal jumped into his car and hurtled down the street.

He stopped again and looked over his shoulder.

The jar suddenly exploded.

The appendix shot into the air. It turned over and over like a drunken bird.

The appendix was free.

FIVE

Back at the school Trevor struggled to get away from Mr Birtle. But the teacher was too strong. Trevor fought like a wild thing but it was no good. He couldn't slip out of Mr Birtle's iron grip.

Suddenly his body slumped. Lifeless. He drooped like a rag doll in Mr Birtle's arms. Mr Birtle lowered him to the floor. He placed his ear to Trevor's chest. Then he rushed to the cupboard for a rug.

Trevor leapt up and sprinted out of the school. His trick had worked. He was free.

Free to find his appendix.

And the appendix was free to find him. It slithered along the empty footpath like a wet, foul mouse.

There was not a person to be seen. Only a cat. A large ginger cat. It saw the appendix and it liked what it saw. With one quick spring the cat jumped down from its perch on a fence.

It landed right in front of the appendix.

The appendix stopped.

The cat crouched low.

The appendix quivered. The cat dabbed at the wobbling shape. Its paw seemed to stick to the appendix.

The cat gave three terrified squeals.

'Miaow, miaow, miaow.'

Then it vanished into the appendix.

Sucked up like a rag into a vacuum cleaner. It disappeared as easily and noisily as jelly slurped up a straw. The appendix shivered and continued its journey. It was no bigger. It was no smaller. But it had eaten the cat.

47

Suddenly the appendix started squealing.

'*Miaow, miaow, miaow.*'

The appendix copied the cat's last cries. Down the street it went, squealing in a tiny voice.

'*Miaow, miaow, miaow,*' it squealed.

The appendix rounded a corner and stopped again. An angry dog barred the way. It yapped and flapped and circled the bit of slimy gut that quivered before it.

Suddenly the appendix moved. In a flash it leapt up and fixed itself to the dog's ear. The dog yelped in agony. It tried to shake off the appendix.

'Ruff, ruff, ruff.'

Too late it realised its mistake.

The appendix slurped.

And sucked up the dog without so much as a burp. The dog was gone. Vanished. And the appendix, still small and foul, slithered on its way.

'Ruff, ruff, ruff,' yipped the appendix. It copied its last meal's voice. Over and over.

'Ruff, ruff, ruff.'

It seemed to enjoy the sound of the dog it had eaten for dinner.

Across the road slithered the awful piece of slime. Under a car and down a drain. It seemed to know where it was going.

It did know where it was going.

It was heading for Trevor.

'Squeak, squeak, squeak.'

By now, Trevor had run a long way from the school. He panted and looked behind him. There was no one following. He had escaped. But he was out of breath. His head hurt. His hands were damp with sweat.

But he felt a little better.

Somehow he knew that the appendix was on its way. It would never leave him. He sat down in the gutter and waited.

Next to a drain.

'*Squeak, squeak, squeak.*' A tiny cry. The appendix slithered out of the drain, still imitating its last meal. A meal that it had met in the drain. A rat that had been just a little too curious.

Trevor smiled when he saw the appendix. 'We must always be together,' he said.

The appendix seemed to agree. It slithered up Trevor's leg. Over his jumper. Up his neck. On to his chin.

Trevor opened his mouth very wide.

'We must always be together,' he said.

There was a gulp.

And they were.

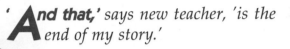

'**And that,**' says new teacher, 'is the end of my story.'

A shiver goes down my spine. I wish I could stop peering at the thing in the jar.

All the kids in the class sit and stare in silence at the jar on Mr Denton's desk. The horrible grey thing circles silently in the yellow fluid.

'What do you think?' says Mr Denton.

The kids are feeling a bit sick. It's a good story but not one to cheer you up. Everyone claps politely just as the bell rings. The class files out for lunch but no one walks anywhere near the horrible grey thing in the jar.

56

I hang back until they are all gone. I want to talk to the new teacher about his story.

'There is one thing wrong with that story,' I say.

'Yes?' says Mr Denton.

'If that appendix was swallowed by Trevor,' I say, 'how come it is still in the jar on your desk?'

Mr Denton scratches his chin. 'You've got me there,' he says. 'It is a bit of a weakness in the story. But I can't tell you what really happened.'

'Why not?' I say.

'It was too horrible,' he says.

'You can tell me,' I say.

'Sorry,' says Mr Denton. 'But you would never believe me anyway.'

'It's only a story,' I say. 'Isn't it?'

'Is it?' says Mr Denton. He smiles at me and goes off for lunch.

58

The jar has something floating around inside it. Something awful. Something grey and fleshy. Something foul. Something not alive but not dead either.

A shiver goes down my spine. I wish I could stop peering at the thing in the jar.

But I can't.

I decide to take off the lid and have a good look. The lid is on tight. I can't budge it. I pull open Mr Denton's desk drawer and find a rag.

I twist the top of the jar with the rag and it starts to move. I twist and twist until finally the lid is off.

I look inside the jar. The slimy bit of flesh does not move.

Not at first.

Then, slowly, horribly, it slides out of the jar.

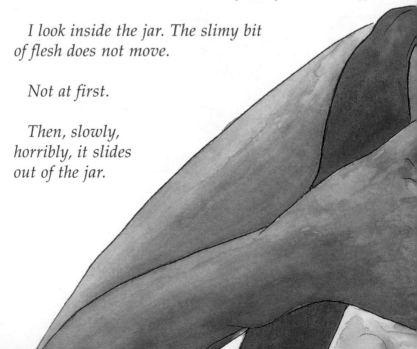

It speaks in the words of its last meal.

'We must always be together,'
it says in a tiny voice.

'We must always
be together.'

'We must always be together.'

'We must always be together.'

Mr Jennings!!!

So he's the most POPULAR children's author
in Australia, is he? Thinks that when I draw dogs
they look like sacks of wheat with legs on, does he?
Writes a book about an appendix when he knows
I was attacked by one as a child!!!

It wasn't my fault that I backed over him with my car.
So he has a few broken bones… what about my car?
It's a mess.

But there's no hard feelings.
In fact I'm taking him for
a little walk to see the cliff-top view….

…from the bottom.

T.D.

Publisher's note: Mr Denton is now under medication
and resting in a home for overworked illustrators.

Mr Denton!!!

Talk about ungrateful. I put him in my story and change his personality into a nice one and what do I get? He does an ugly drawing of me and then tries to push me over a cliff.

Fair suck of the sauce bottle. This is no good. I will not sit for it. If anyone is going to be taken for a ride it will not be me. Where's the scissors? I'll fix him.

Wants to be POPULAR, does he? Okay, I will see to it that he makes a big splash.

I just hope he can swim.

P.J.

Publisher's note: The home for overworked illustrators[1] closed down due to a shortage of patients. They only had one – and he was faking it.

[1]Oxymoron